CEDAR PARK PUBLIC LIBRARY
5 4161 00105536 2

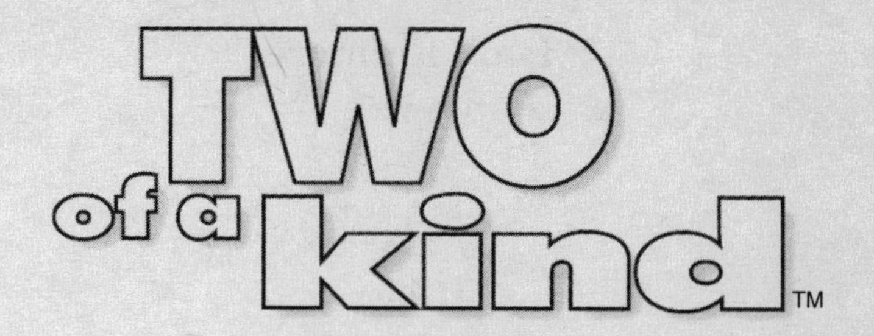

Likes Me, Likes Me Not

Look for more

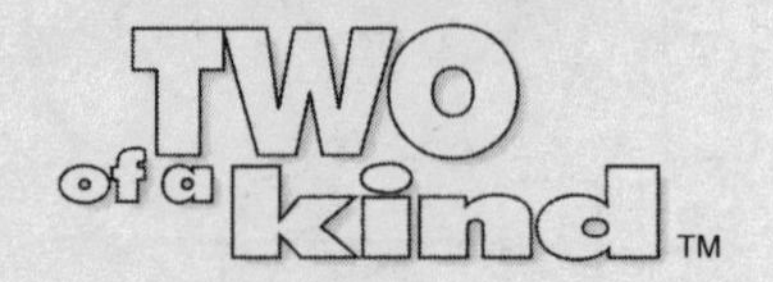

titles:

#1 It's a Twin Thing
#2 How to Flunk Your First Date
#3 The Sleepover Secret
#4 One Twin Too Many
#5 To Snoop or Not to Snoop
#6 My Sister the Supermodel
#7 Two's a Crowd
#8 Let's Party!
#9 Calling All Boys
#10 Winner Take All
#11 P.S. Wish You Were Here
#12 The Cool Club
#13 War of the Wardrobes
#14 Bye-bye Boyfriend
#15 It's Snow Problem

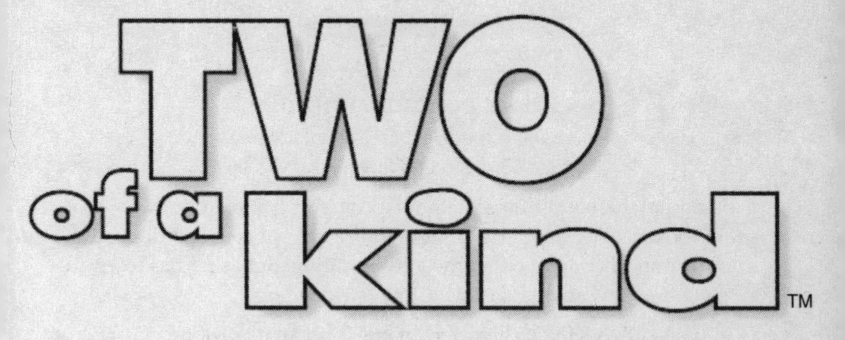

Likes Me, Likes Me Not

by Megan Stine

from the series created by
Robert Griffard
& Howard Adler

HarperEntertainment
An Imprint of HarperCollins*Publishers*

A PARACHUTE PRESS BOOK

A PARACHUTE PRESS BOOK

Parachute Publishing, L.L.C.
156 Fifth Avenue
Suite 302
New York, NY 10010

Published by
HarperEntertainment
An Imprint of HarperCollins*Publishers*
10 East 53rd Street, New York, NY 10022

TWO OF A KIND books created and produced by Parachute Press, L.C.C., in cooperation with Dualstar Publications, a division of Dualstar Entertainment Group, Inc., published by HarperEntertainment, an imprint of HarperCollins Publishers.

For information address HarperCollins Publishers, 10 East 53rd Street, New York, NY 10022.

ISBN 0-06-106656-7

First printing: April 2001

Printed in the United States of America

Visit HarperEntertainment on the World Wide Web at www.harpercollins.com

10 9 8 7 6 5 4 3

CHAPTER ONE

"You're kidding!" Mary-Kate Burke said to her sister, Ashley. "This place? We're supposed to have our Spring Fling dance in here?"

"Not just the Spring Fling dance," Samantha Kramer chimed in. "They think we're going to be spending all our free time here! Welcome to the new Student Union for White Oak Academy and Harrington."

"But it's just a storage building!" Mary-Kate complained. "It's dark, it's grungy, it's smelly, and . . . and . . . I think I saw a mouse!"

"A mouse? Yuk! Where!" Dana Woletsky screeched.

"It went under there," Mary-Kate said, pointing

to a pile of old mattresses in the corner.

Ashley gazed around at the dusty storage building. She didn't see the mouse. But her sister was right—it was dark and grungy. And smelly.

Well, at least it's big, Ashley thought.

And the reason it was dark was because so much stuff was piled in front of the windows. The place was filled to the brim with old chairs and mattresses, boxes, out-of-date textbooks, broken brooms, and rusty old gardening equipment.

Once it's cleaned out, Ashley realized, *it's going to be a nice big space. With a little paint, some new furniture, lights, and a sound system, it could be a great Student Union.*

The storage building was on the property of White Oak Academy—the New Hampshire boarding school that Ashley and Mary-Kate attended. Right next door was the Harrington School for Boys. The new Student U was going to be used by the First and Second Forms in both schools. That's what the seventh and eighth grades were called.

In other words, it was a dream come true as far as Ashley was concerned. The guys and the girls were going to be able to hang out together all the time—not just on the few days when they had the same classes.

Ashley was the head of the girls' committee in charge of fixing up the old building.

"Trust me," she said. "When I get done with it, this place is going to look fabulous!"

"Well, you're the boss," Samantha said. "Where do we start?"

"Just grab some stuff and start hauling it out," Ashley said. "Mr. Frangianella will be here pretty soon to show us which stuff is trash and which is treasure."

"You mean we're supposed to touch that mess?" Dana Woletsky asked. "I just had my nails done." She wrinkled up her nose and made a face.

Trust Dana to start complaining right away, Ashley thought. Dana was snooty and usually acted like she owned the whole school. She obviously thought she was the queen of the First Form.

"If you want to be on the committee, you've got to work," Ashley said.

"Fine," Dana said, inching toward a pile of boxes. "But what about the mouse?"

"A mouse? Cool. Where?" a boy's voice called out.

Ashley whirled around. A group of guys from Harrington were standing in the open doorway. They were going to help clean up the Student U, too.

"Where's the mouse?" Grant Marino repeated.

Ashley glanced at her sister and saw Mary-Kate blush. Mary-Kate used to have a real crush on Grant. "It ran under there." Mary-Kate pointed to the mattresses again.

"Forget the mouse," Ross Lambert said. "Let's start hauling this junk out of here."

Grant and Marty Silver moved toward the pile of stuff. "I'll be with you guys in a moment," Ross continued. "Just as soon as I have a talk with Ashley."

Ross wants to talk to me? Ashley thought. *Maybe he wants to ask me to the Spring Fling dance!*

Her heart skipped a beat.

Ross was the first guy Ashley had a crush on when she came to White Oak. He had big brown eyes, sandy brown hair, and dimples. She was always a sucker for dimples.

Ashley knew Ross liked her, too. Sometimes they went out for pizza or to a movie. She even went to her first big dance with him. Ashley thought of Ross as her sort-of boyfriend.

Ashley pushed her long blond hair out of her eyes and smiled at him. "What's up?" she asked, trying to sound casual.

"We're supposed to talk about the Student U," Ross explained. "I'm the chairman of the boys' committee."

Oh. Ashley's heart sank for an instant. *He only wants to talk about the Student U,* she thought. *Not about the dance. Maybe he hasn't thought about it yet.*

But then she realized that if he was chairman of the boys' committee, they'd be working together full time for the next two weeks!

"Let's check this place out," Ross said, marching through the crowded storage building. He headed toward some smaller rooms at the back. Ashley followed him.

"This is just a closet," Ross said. He opened a door and closed it again.

"We can store decorations for the dances in there," Ashley said.

"Yeah, or build a shelf and use it for all the video games," Ross suggested.

Then he ducked into the back room. It was small and private. "This will be great for a game room," Ross said.

"Or a cozy little lounge," Ashley suggested. "Can't you just picture it? Sofas, low tables, stuffed chairs. Like a coffee bar, but without the espresso machine. And maybe we could put one of the TVs in here."

Ross frowned. "Whatever," he said as he slid past her, back into the main room.

Hey, it was just an idea! Ashley thought, following him.

Ross pushed past the pile of mattresses. Ashley kept her arms held tightly at her sides. She was on mouse alert.

At the other end of the building, they found another small room. Boxes were piled up in front of a door leading outside.

Ross glanced at her. "How about a game room here?" he suggested, raising his eyebrows.

Maybe, Ashley thought. "Or a kitchenette," she said. "We could put a microwave in here, and the drink and candy machines. That way the food won't clutter up the big room."

"Well, where are we going to put the video games?" Ross asked. "You don't want them in the back, you don't want them up here. . . "

"Hey, we'll find a place," Ashley assured him. "I was just brainstorming, okay?"

"That's the right word for it," Dana Woletsky commented loudly from the other room. "Ashley's brain is always in a storm!"

Dana's best friend Kristin Lindquist laughed.

Ross laughed, too. "Besides," he went on, "I don't know if we've got the money for a microwave. Not after we buy two VCRs and about a zillion video games."

Ashley frowned and thought about their budget.

Ross was right—they couldn't buy everything they wanted. The two schools were going to supply all the major stuff—new furniture, vending machines, two TVs and a portable Ping-Pong table. But the student committees had a small budget. Ashley and Ross were supposed to decide how to spend it.

"Two VCRs?" Ashley argued. "Why do we need two? I thought we'd use our budget to get a sound system, strobe lights, and a mirrored disco ball for the Spring Fling."

"Oh, man, no way," Ross shot back. He shook his head. "Strobe lights are cool, but you can only use them at dances about twice a year. But if we get two VCRs, we can watch two different movies at the same time all year round." He paused. "On the other hand . . ."

Ross marched back into the main room and looked around. "You might have a point," he said, nodding. "Strobe lights might look really cool in here with the walls painted black."

"Black?" Ashley's voice rose. "Are you kidding?"

"Okay, red and black," Ross compromised.

Ashley gulped. "Uh, I was seeing this room in softer colors," she argued. "Like maybe peach and pastel seafoam green."

"Ick." Ross made a face. "Peach is a wussy color."

"Look," Ashley said. "I know that the Student U is for White Oak and Harrington. But we're probably going to be using it more than you guys, since it's on White Oak property. And we're having the Lock-In here—the same night as the dance. So I think the girls should have more say about what colors we paint the walls. It's only fair."

"What's a Lock-In?" Ross asked.

"It's so cool!" Dana said, dropping everything and rushing over to butt in on the conversation. "It's an all-night slumber party, just for the First- and Second-Form girls! We get to bring our pillows and sleeping bags, and they're going to lock us in here. . . ."

"With the mouse," Grant Marino interrupted. He shot Mary-Kate a secret smile, but Ashley saw it.

Wow, Ashley thought. *He's flirting with Mary-Kate! I'll bet he likes her.*

"Don't interrupt," Dana said. "Anyway, we get to stay up all Saturday night watching videos, playing games, and eating junk food. . . ."

"And then at, like, six in the morning on Sunday, we go back to our dorms to sleep," Ashley jumped back in.

"Cool," Max Dorfman said. "Maybe we'll come over and raid the place."

"Not a bad idea," Samantha encouraged him.

"So, don't you see?" Ashley insisted. "I mean, about the paint colors?"

Ross shrugged. "We can argue about that later," he said. "First we've got to get this place cleaned out."

He picked up a stack of folding chairs and headed for the door. Ashley grabbed a mattress and started dragging it. It was pretty heavy.

"Okay," she called after him. "But I have an idea."

Ross put the chairs down on the lawn outside. Then he came back to give Ashley a hand. He lifted one end of the mattress.

"What?" he asked.

"We should have a fund-raiser," Ashley suggested. "That way, maybe we'll have enough money for the strobe lights and the VCR *and* the video games. We can get everything."

"That's the smartest thing you've said all day," Ross said. He gave her a half-smile. Half—because only one of his two dimples showed.

"Great!" Ashley said. "We'll have a bake sale!"

"Bake sale? You don't want to eat the brownies I'd bake, believe me," Ross joked. "How about a pizza sale?"

"No." Ashley shook her head. "We had a pizza sale for the chorus last month, and we only made fifty dollars. How about if we offer to walk dogs for all the teachers who live on campus?"

"Not enough teachers have dogs," Ross said in a grouchy tone. "Look—do whatever you want. Just let me know, and I'll make sure my guys show up."

He yanked the mattress away from her and threw it on the trash pile. Then he glanced at his watch. "I've got to go," he said. "I've got a paper to write for history. Catch you later."

Wait! Ashley thought. *Don't go away angry!*

But it was too late. Ross was already hiking toward the shuttle bus that would take him back to Harrington.

I really blew it, she thought. *That whole conversation went wrong. I want to do it over!*

She watched Ross run across the green. But at the last minute, just before he hopped on the bus, he turned around and waved at her. And smiled.

Ashley's heart skipped a beat.

Maybe he still likes me after all, Ashley thought. *And if he does, maybe we'll be going together to the Spring Fling!*

CHAPTER TWO

"Where should we sit?" Mary-Kate said. She gazed around the dining hall with her lunch tray in her hands.

"All the tables are full," Ashley answered. "Except that one."

She nodded toward the only table with empty chairs. It was the one where Dana Woletsky and her friends were sitting.

Mary-Kate shrugged. "I guess we don't have a choice." She hurried over and plopped her tray down—at the other end of the table from where Dana was sitting. After working all morning, cleaning out the storage building, she and Mary-Kate were both starved.

"So tell me everything," Mary-Kate said after she'd taken a few bites. "You and Ross spent a lot of time together in those small back rooms. What's up between you two?

Ashley chewed her French bread before answering. Then she leaned close to her sister.

"I like working with him," she said softly. "But he was being a pain. He didn't like any of my ideas."

"Like what?" Mary-Kate asked.

"Like my plan to get a sound system for the Student U!" Ashley complained. "He wants a second VCR instead. Can you believe that? How does he think we're supposed to have the Spring Fling dance without music?"

"I don't know," Mary-Kate said.

Ashley shrugged. "Anyway, he was really hard to work with," she said.

"Wow," Mary-Kate said. "I wonder why."

Dana Woletsky stood up at the other end of the table and looked right at Ashley. "If you can't get along with Ross," she said, "did you ever think maybe you're the problem? I mean, he's the sweetest guy in the whole world. At least he's always been extremely sweet to me."

"Hey," Mary-Kate blurted out. "This is a private conversation."

"I'm just trying to give you some much-needed advice, Ashley," Dana said. "All I'm saying is that you're much too bossy. Anyone would find it hard to work with you."

Bossy? Ashley thought. *Look who's calling who bossy.*

Dana picked up her tray and walked away. Fiona and Kristin trailed after her.

Ashley stared at them.

"I'm not too bossy, am I?" Ashley asked when they were gone.

"Define too bossy," Mary-Kate joked.

"Thanks a lot." Ashley rolled her eyes.

"No, really—you're good at organizing things," Mary-Kate said. "That's why the Head picked you to be in charge of the Student U committee—right?"

The Head was their nickname for Mrs. Pritchard. She was the headmistress at White Oak Academy.

"Right," Ashley agreed.

"Well, maybe Ross is good at organizing things, too," Mary-Kate said logically. "So both of you want to run the show, and you end up getting on each other's nerves. You know—it's like too many cooks in the kitchen or something."

"I don't know what to think," Ashley said as they left the dining hall. "I only know I like Ross—and I want him to like me back!"

The twins strolled across the lawn, back toward their dorm, Porter House. It was a beautiful, cool, spring day in New Hampshire. Crocuses poked up through the grass.

"Hey! Ashley! Wait up!" a voice called.

Ashley stopped and saw Phoebe Cahill running toward them. Phoebe was Ashley's roommate. She was wearing a pair of bright paisley bell-bottom pants and a cute little bright orange top. Vintage, of course. Most of Phoebe's clothes were from another decade.

"Hey, Phoebe," Ashley called. "Let me ask you something. I'm not too bossy, am I?"

"What do you mean by too bossy?" Phoebe asked.

"Ha ha!" Mary-Kate teased. "I told you so."

"Stop it!" Ashley blushed. "Anyway, Mary-Kate already made that joke."

"Okay—you're not too bossy," Phoebe said. "Is that what you want to hear?"

"No, I want the truth," Ashley said.

"Well, the truth is, I'm bored!" Phoebe said, changing the subject. "What are we going to do today?"

"How about a trip to the mall?" Mary-Kate suggested.

"Too late," Phoebe said. "We just missed the bus."

"I know!" Ashley's face lit up. "How about if we rearrange the furniture in our room? Mary-Kate, you can help. We'll move our bunk beds to the window, so we can look outside while we're lying in bed. Then we'll push our desks to where the dressers are. And put one dresser on each side of the door. Your posters can go on the closet door, Phoebe. And the wastebaskets can go beside the bed. What do you think?"

Mary-Kate and Phoebe both burst out laughing.

"You? Bossy?" Phoebe teased. "No way. Just tell me where you want me to put my toothbrush!"

Ashley frowned. "Hey, no fair! I was just trying to think of something to do, since neither of you could decide."

"Okay." Phoebe smiled. "Anyway, moving the furniture sounds like a plan. It'll be fun."

"Easy for you to say," Mary-Kate joked. "You haven't been hauling trash out of the storage building all morning!"

"Look at it this way," Ashley told her sister. "At least you're already dressed for it. You don't have to change into old clothes!"

"Fine," Mary-Kate said as they climbed the stairs toward their rooms. "But I still want to stop in my room and ask Campbell . . ."

She stared into her dorm room and gasped. Ashley peeked her head in, too.

The room looked different. It took Ashley a moment to figure out why. All of Campbell Smith's stuff was gone. Her posters . . . her clothes . . . her sports trophies . . . her bedspread . . . her stuffed animals . . .

All gone.

And Campbell was gone, too. Someone brand new was sitting on her bed instead!

"Hi," the girl said, smiling at Mary-Kate. "I'm your new roommate."

CHAPTER THREE

"New roommate?" Mary-Kate gulped. "What happened to Campbell?"

"She and I had to trade rooms," the girl said. "I'm Ginger. Ginger Halliday. I hope you don't mind."

Mind? Mary-Kate thought. *Uh . . . yeah. I mind. I mind a lot! I like Campbell.*

"Uh, I just didn't know they did that at White Oak," Mary-Kate stammered. "I mean, change roommates in the middle of the year."

Mary-Kate glanced at her sister and Phoebe, who were still there. Ashley looked just as shocked as Mary-Kate felt.

"It was sort of sudden," Ginger said. "Campbell

just moved out fifteen minutes ago."

"So is Campbell gone for good?" Ashley asked.

"Only for a few weeks—probably," Ginger said. She turned her head away and coughed. Then she brushed her bright red bangs out of her eyes. "I have a bunch of allergies," she went on. "And I've been sick a lot this year. My doctors think maybe I'm allergic to something in my dorm room—or maybe to my roommate! Wouldn't that be funny?"

"Well, you'll definitely be allergic to Mary-Kate by the time you're done," Ashley joked. "She gets under *my* skin, anyway."

"Ha ha," Mary-Kate said weakly.

But secretly she thought: *This isn't funny!*

She didn't want a new roommate. She wanted Campbell back! Campbell was a lot like Mary-Kate—good at sports and a straight-talker. The two of them had become really good friends.

"So you're moving in here?" Phoebe asked. "And Campbell moved into your room?"

Ginger nodded. "I was living in Phipps," she said. Phipps was the dorm next door to Porter House. "Campbell's my friend. When she heard I was sick, she offered to help out."

"What do you mean it's only for a few weeks?" Mary-Kate asked.

"Well, my doctor wants to try this for awhile,"

Ginger said. "If my allergies clear up, then maybe he's right. Maybe I am allergic to my roommate! Or to her hand lotion or something. I don't know. We'll see."

Mary-Kate gulped and glanced at Ashley again. They both knew what that meant. If Ginger's allergies disappeared, then maybe she'd have to stay in Mary-Kate's room. Then Campbell would never come back.

"Wow," Mary-Kate said. "This happened so . . . so fast."

She tried to smile at Ginger.

It's not her fault, Mary-Kate thought, trying to be nice to the new girl.

"My doctor just decided last night," Ginger said.

"Oh." Mary-Kate couldn't think of anything else to say.

"Uh, look," Ashley said. "Maybe you guys want to get to know each other. Why don't you just hang out here, Mary-Kate? Phoebe and I will go move our furniture ourselves."

"Yes, boss-woman," Phoebe joked, bowing to Ashley.

Mary-Kate laughed. "Thanks," she said. "I'll see you later."

Ashley and Phoebe wandered down the hall to their room.

"I put my clothes in the closet," Ginger went on. "I had to hang a piece of plastic between your clothes and mine—just in case. Hope you don't mind."

"In case what?" Mary-Kate asked. "I have cooties?"

Ginger sort of shrugged and smiled. "I don't know. My doctor told me to do it."

She hopped off her bed—Campbell's bed—and grabbed a tissue to blow her nose. Then she stuck an inhaler in her mouth and breathed in the medication.

Mary-Kate checked her out quickly while her back was turned.

Ginger had very pale skin and was so thin she was almost bony. Freckles dotted her face and arms. She was wearing a pair of baggy blue jeans and a rust-colored sweatshirt, with the sleeves pushed up.

"Who was your roommate?" Mary-Kate asked.

"In Phipps? Oh, Jamie Randolph," Ginger answered.

Mary-Kate waited for Ginger to go on, but she didn't.

"So are you two close? I mean, are you sorry you had to move here?" Mary-Kate asked.

"She's okay," Ginger said.

She's not much of a conversationalist, Mary-Kate thought.

CHAPTER FOUR

"Ashley! I made it! I made the team!" Mary-Kate called, running across campus the next day.

Ashley whirled around. "What team?"

"The White Oak/Harrington Co-ed All-Stars Baseball team!" Mary-Kate blurted out fast. She shot her fist into the air, in a cheer. "We're going to play Danville Day School in a few weeks."

Ashley smiled and gave her sister a hug. "Way to go," she said. "But you're the super-jock. You always make the A-teams."

Yeah, Mary-Kate thought. *I do. So why am I so super-excited?*

She knew the answer in a heartbeat. In fact, she knew it the minute she had walked into the gym that morning and saw the names on the list of players.

Grant was going to be on the All-Stars team, too!

"It's just going to be such a blast," Mary-Kate said. "We start practicing as a team next week."

"Cool," Ashley said. "But you're still going to help out with the Student U, aren't you?"

"Oh, I can't wait to haul more dirty mattresses," Mary-Kate joked. "Just pile 'em on."

"Listen, I'm going over there now," Ashley said. "We still have a few boxes to move, and some old pipes to haul out. And we've got to sweep the floor. Some of the guys are meeting us. Can you come?"

"Why not?" Mary-Kate said. "I can't think of a better way to avoid homework—or Ginger."

Ashley shot her sister a glance. "You don't like her?" Ashley asked.

"I guess she's okay," Mary-Kate said. "I mean, she's nice enough—but she's definitely not Campbell. And she keeps asking me if I like Grant. It's really annoying!"

"Well, do you?" Ashley said.

"Don't you start, too!" Mary-Kate complained.

"I was just wondering," Ashley said. "Because there he is!" She nodded toward the storage building.

Mary-Kate's head snapped around. There, in the distance, she saw the guys from the Harrington committee: Ross, Grant, Marty Silver, David Friel, and Elliot Smith.

Her face lit up.

"So you do still like him!" Ashley said.

"Yes. But don't tell anyone," Mary-Kate whispered. "I don't want it all over the school, like last time!"

"Okay," Ashley agreed.

The girls started walking a little faster. When they reached the storage shed, the guys just stared at them.

Mary-Kate and Ashley stared back.

"What are you waiting for?" Ashley asked. "Let's go in."

"Who has the key?" Ross asked.

"Oh! Sorry," Ashley said. She reached into her pocket, pulled out the key, and unlocked the storage building.

Mary-Kate hung back, waiting to see what Grant would do. He shot her a smile. "You coming in?" he said. "Or are you afraid your sister is going to lock us all in here together?"

I wish! Mary-Kate thought.

"Whoa!" Elliot hooted. "Grant wants to go to the girls' Lock-In!"

"Don't forget to bring your nightie!" David teased him.

Grant smacked David on the arm and body-slammed Elliot. The other guys just laughed.

"So what are we here for?" Elliot asked as they stepped inside.

Mary-Kate looked around. The big storage room was still dirty, but it was almost empty. They had practically finished cleaning it out yesterday.

"The boxes in the back room go into the Dumpster outside," Ashley said, giving out orders.

"We'll get those," David said, motioning two guys to come with him.

"And those pipes," Ashley said. "They go out. And we've got to sweep."

"I'll sweep," Mary-Kate offered, quickly grabbing a broom. It sounded easier than hauling old cast-iron pipes.

"Thanks," Ashley said. "Ross and I should talk about the fund-raiser anyway."

Ross rolled his eyes, but he followed Ashley outside. The two of them sat under a tree, talking.

"You need some help?" Grant asked Mary-Kate.

"What—you mean I should give you half the broom?" she joked.

"I guess that won't work," he said, sort of shrugging. He hopped up onto a wide windowsill and sat dangling his legs.

Mary-Kate kept sweeping. Marty and Elliot

marched through the room with the few remaining boxes.

"You look like you're dancing with that thing," Marty teased her.

"Ahhh!" Elliot laughed. "Mary-Kate's date for the Spring Fling! A broom!"

"Very funny," Mary-Kate snapped, but they were already outside.

"Hey—ignore them," Grant said. "I'll bet you'll have a better date than that stupid broom."

"You think so?" Mary-Kate asked.

Grant nodded and shot her a shy smile.

I think he's flirting with me! Mary-Kate thought. Her heart started pounding a mile a minute.

"I don't know," she said. "I mean, the broom asked me first."

Grant laughed. "The broom's too tall for you," he said. "You need someone more your size."

Wow! Mary-Kate realized. *He* is *flirting!*

Was he trying to ask her for a date?

"Hey, did you see we're both on the All-Stars team?" he said.

"Yeah." She nodded.

"Well, I was thinking that maybe we could—" he started to say.

But Ross interrupted.

"Grant-man! Get a move on and haul those pipes!" Ross yelled, poking his head back into the storage building.

"Okay, okay," Grant grumbled.

He hopped off the window and picked up the pipes with a groan. A minute later, the other guys joined him.

Bummer! Mary-Kate thought. *Why did Ross have to butt in right then? He almost asked me out. At least I think he was going to.*

"You kids about done?" Mr. Frangianella stepped into the building. "I'm supposed to be watching you, but I've got some bushes that need trimming."

"Okay. Two secs," Mary-Kate said.

Quickly she finished sweeping, then hurried outside. Mr. Frangianella took the key back from Ashley and locked the building up. The Harrington guys wandered off to get the shuttle bus to their campus.

"Won't it be nice when the Student U is done?" Ashley said. "I mean, the guys won't always have to rush away. They can hang around here all weekend!"

"I know," Mary-Kate said dreamily.

She stared at Grant, watching him leave. His hair looked cute, even from the back!

"Hi," a voice behind Mary-Kate said. "What's up?"

Mary-Kate turned. Ginger had come up behind them.

"Hi," Mary-Kate said. "Not much. Just working on the new Student U."

"With Grant Marino?" Ginger said, grinning widely.

Mary-Kate gave Ginger a blank stare. What was she doing? Trying to dig up some more gossip?

"Yeah, he was there. And a bunch of other guys," Mary-Kate said.

"So does that mean you like him?" Ginger asked eagerly.

Give me a break! Mary-Kate thought. *Can't she think of anything else to talk about?*

"No way," Mary-Kate insisted.

Ginger shrugged. "Okay. Just asking," she said. "I've got to go." She turned and walked away.

"What's that about?" Ashley asked when Ginger was gone.

"She won't stop asking me about Grant," Mary-Kate confessed. "She's driving me nuts."

"I can see that," Ashley observed. "Your face is all red! But why don't you just tell her the truth?"

"I was totally embarrassed in front of Grant once before!" Mary-Kate complained. "It's not going to happen again."

Ashley winced. Mary-Kate knew what her sister was thinking. The rumors last time were all Ashley's fault.

"Well, I'm not saying a word this time," Ashley promised.

"Good," Mary-Kate said. "Me, either."

Not until I know for sure if I stand a chance with Grant!

CHAPTER FIVE

"Don't look now," Ashley whispered to her sister. "But here he comes."

"Who?" Mary-Kate whirled around.

"Grant!" *And here comes Ross, too!* Ashley added silently. She felt her heart start to skip a beat.

It was another beautiful Saturday, a week later. They were holding a car wash to raise money for the new Student U. Ashley and Mary-Kate and a bunch of other girls had been washing cars all morning—and waiting for the guys to show up.

"Shhh!" Mary-Kate said. "I don't even think I like him anymore. He's been ignoring me at baseball practice all week."

"Really?" Ashley's eyes opened wide. "Last

Saturday he acted like he was nuts about you."

"I know," Mary-Kate replied. "It's making me crazy. Does he like me—or doesn't he?"

Ashley shrugged. "Who knows," she said. "But if you care, you have soapsuds in your hair."

Both girls pretended to get busy with the buckets, soap, and towels. Out of the corner of her eye, Ashley watched Ross and Grant walking toward them.

"Hi," Mary-Kate said when Grant was near.

"Hi," he answered flatly. "Your hair's full of soap."

"So I've heard," Mary-Kate said. She reached back and scooped off a handful of suds. "Want some?" She held it out like whipped cream.

"No thanks," Grant said, turning away. He picked up a towel and started drying one of the washed cars.

Mary-Kate's right! Ashley thought. *He's changed completely from last week. Now he's barely speaking to her.*

She saw Mary-Kate's face fall.

I know how you feel, Ashley thought. Ross wasn't paying much attention to her, either.

Ross picked up the hose and started goofing off with it. He pretended he was going to squirt Dana Woletsky.

"If you get me wet, I swear I'll make you pay!" Dana teased Ross.

"Yeah? How much?" he taunted her.

"I'll think about it," Dana warned him, flashing her best smile.

"Ross, we've got to talk," Ashley said, interrupting them.

"What's up?" he asked.

"Well," Ashley said, "we still haven't decided how to spend the money for the Student U. And we've got to buy the paint. They're going to start painting tomorrow."

Ross shrugged and tossed the hose to the ground. "Whatever you want," he said.

"Really?" Ashley's eyes lit up. "You mean you're okay with painting the walls peach and green?"

"Whoa!" Ross said. "I didn't say peach. I'm thinking compromise. How about one black wall at least? And you can paint the other three that seafoam color, or whatever you call it."

"Now we're getting somewhere!" Ashley said, beaming.

"Oh, come on," Dana said, butting in. "Black and seafoam green? That's yucky."

"Yeah," Elliot called. "You know—the colors of rotting flesh."

Ross, Grant, Elliot, and Dana all laughed.

"I think one black wall could look really cool with three seafoam walls," Ashley insisted.

Dana muttered something under her breath, but Ashley didn't hear what it was.

Ross laughed again.

Why doesn't she just go away? Ashley thought.

"About the money," Ashley went on, trying to get back to the main topic. "Maybe we should go somewhere and talk about it—in private."

Ashley shot a glance at Dana, hoping she'd get the message.

"What's to talk about?" Ross asked.

"The disco lights, for one," Ashley started to say. "Everyone wants them. So I was thinking . . . "

"Okay, okay," Ross said, interrupting. "If you really want the disco lights, that's cool with me. I mean, I don't want half the female population of White Oak mad at me for ruining the dance or something."

"Really?" Ashley's face lit up again.

"Oooh, you've made her soooo happy," Dana sniped in a mocking tone.

A moment later, a teacher from Harrington pulled up in his white Toyota. "Can I get this washed right away?" he called out.

"Of course!" Ashley said. She handed Ross a bucket of soapy water. "Here," she said. "You soap the front. I'll scrub the tires."

Ashley walked around to the far side of the car with a big sponge and another bucket. She bent down to soap the hubcaps.

"Honestly, Ross," she called. "You won't be sorry about the disco lights. And besides—I've been thinking about how we could get the extra VCR that you wanted. If we make enough money . . ."

But before Ashley could finish her sentence, a whole bucket of soapy water flew over the car.

It landed right on her head, drenching her.

"Hey!" Ashley cried, jumping up.

Too late. She was a drippy, soaking mess. Her clothes stuck to her, and her hair hung like strings, plastered to her face.

Ross burst out laughing.

"What was that for?" Ashley snapped at him.

But then she saw that Ross wasn't holding the bucket.

Dana was!

Dana smiled. "Oops," she said. "I didn't see you over there. Sorry. You're so small."

"Very funny," Ashley said, shivering.

It was a warm day for April in New Hampshire.

But not that warm. Not warm enough to stay outside in sopping wet clothes.

"L-l-listen," she said to Ross, her teeth chattering. "I'm going to g-g-go change. Maybe we can talk about this at lunch."

"Okay," Ross said with a shrug.

Ashley hurried back to her dorm and changed as quickly as she could. Then she ran back across campus, to the car wash. But as she neared the spot, her heart sank. Most of the guys had left.

"Where did Ross go?" Ashley asked Mary-Kate.

"He went to eat lunch," Mary-Kate answered. "And I hate to tell you who went with him. Dana!"

Oh, no! Ashley thought.

Dana is trying to ruin things between me and Ross!

If she keeps this up, he'll never go to the dance with me. Never.

CHAPTER SIX

"Campbell! Hi!" Mary-Kate called across the dining hall that night.

Mary-Kate had just come out of the cafeteria line with her dinner tray. Mrs. Pritchard was on her way in. She gave Mary-Kate a frown.

"Mary-Kate, please try to wait until your friend is within earshot," the Head said. "That way you won't have to scream at her."

"Sorry, Mrs. Pritchard," Mary-Kate said.

But she couldn't wait to talk to her old roommate. Mary-Kate had hardly seen her since she moved.

"Campbell!" she called again, softer this time.

Campbell waved and pointed to a table. Mary-Kate made her way through the dining hall and sat down. Four other girls from Phipps were already sitting there.

"Hi, stranger!" Mary-Kate said. "I miss you! How's it going in your new dorm?"

"It's okay," Campbell said. "I miss you, too. There's no one I can toss a softball around with."

Mary-Kate beamed.

"Ginger's roommate is funny, though," Campbell went on. "She cracks me up."

"Jamie Randolph? Really? How come?" Mary-Kate asked. She felt a little jealous.

"Oh, she's so klutzy," Campbell said. "I tossed her an apple last night, and she dropped it. But she was hilarious. She started talking in a weird voice as if she was a sports announcer: 'Jamie bobbles the apple for the tenth error of the inning.'"

"Doesn't sound that funny," Mary-Kate said.

"You had to be there," Campbell explained.

"Yeah," Wendy Linden chimed in from the other end of the table. "It was a riot. You should have been there."

I wish I had been, Mary-Kate thought.

She really missed Campbell. Hanging out with Ginger was not much fun.

"Hey—who has a date for the Spring Fling?" Wendy asked.

"I do," one of the girls from Phipps said. "Believe it or not, I'm going with Elliot!"

"You're kidding!" Wendy said. "He asked you?"

The girl nodded.

"Well, I'm going with Danny Strohmeyer," Wendy said.

"Cool," the other girl said.

"But you don't have to have a date—right?" Campbell asked.

"Of course not," Wendy said. "You can just go in a group. Lots of people don't have dates yet, anyway."

Mary-Kate was quiet. She didn't want to talk about this in front of everyone.

"The Lock-In is going to be amazing," Mary-Kate said, hoping to change the subject. "All the movies, pizza, and popcorn we can eat!"

"I wish they'd lock the guys in with us!" a girl said from the far end of the table.

Everyone laughed, and most of the girls agreed.

Campbell leaned closer to Mary-Kate and lowered her voice. "What about you and Ashley?" Campbell asked. "Are you guys going with anyone?"

Mary-Kate shook her head.

But I'm still hoping! she thought.

"Well, I mean, who do you want to go with?" Campbell asked.

Mary-Kate sighed. There was really only one guy she liked right now. And if he didn't like her . . . what was the point?

"I can't think of anyone," Mary-Kate lied. "How about you?"

"Me? Nah. I'd rather go alone, I guess," Campbell said. "But I mean, would you go with Grant if he asked you?"

I can't tell her the truth, Mary-Kate thought. *I can't tell her I like him. Because if Grant doesn't ask me out—I'll look like a loser!*

"No," Mary Kate lied again. "No, I don't think I'd go with Grant. Unless maybe—"

"Campbell!" Wendy interrupted them. "We've got to get going. French class is in two minutes."

"Coming," Campbell said. She shoved a last piece of cake in her mouth. "See you, MK. Let's catch a ball game on TV some night." She hurried out after Wendy.

Mary-Kate was going to explain that Grant hadn't exactly been friendly lately. But Campbell was already gone.

Mary-Kate sighed. Why was everyone so interested in Grant all of a sudden? *I know Campbell isn't interested in him,* she thought.

I wonder if she's asking for Ginger?

CHAPTER SEVEN

"Mary-Kate! You're late!" Coach Fisher called.

"Sorry," Mary-Kate called back as she hurried toward the field for All-Stars practice. "Mrs. Bloomberg kept me after English class."

She grabbed her mitt and ran to take her position in the outfield. Her heart was pounding by the time she got there.

"No, no," Coach Fisher called. "I want you on second base today."

Second base? But that was Grant's position!

Mary-Kate saw Grant's head whip around. He glared at her for half a second.

Oh, great! she thought. *Now he thinks I'm trying to take his spot on the team. He'll hate me forever.*

Grant's head drooped down as he started running toward the outfield.

Her stomach twisted into a knot.

This is no fun, she thought. She used to love baseball. And being on the All-Stars team with Grant was supposed to be the best!

But it was turning out all wrong.

"Shape up, Grant!" the coach called. "We're just trying this out for today. I want the best person for each position. The goal is to win, right?"

"Right," Grant answered weakly from the outfield.

"Come on, Mary-Kate!" Danny yelled, clapping his hands.

For the next hour and a half, Mary-Kate tried to concentrate on baseball. It was hard, though. All she could think about was Grant.

He's right behind me, she thought. *Planning to hate me for the rest of his life.*

When it was Mary-Kate's turn at bat, she couldn't stay focused. She hit a pop fly and was out after only one pitch.

She glanced at Grant for sympathy, but he looked away.

Coach Fisher kept them at practice till 7:00. By then, Mary-Kate was starving. She had to run to get to the dining hall before it closed. She was the only person in there. Everyone else had already eaten—and most of the food was gone.

"Just give me some salad," Mary-Kate said to the woman in the cafeteria.

"Oh, come on, honey," the woman said. "You've got to eat more than that. How about some lasagna?"

For the first time in a month, Mary-Kate felt a twinge of homesickness. The way the cafeteria woman had called her "honey" reminded her of home. Her dad always called her "honey" when he knew she was upset about something.

"Okay," Mary-Kate said. She took the lasagna, sat down, and picked at her food. At least it was still slightly warm.

Shape up, Mary-Kate told herself. *No use getting all pushed out of shape over a boy. Or a dance.*

So what if it was the biggest and most fun dance of the whole school year?

She finished eating, then trudged back to her dorm and dragged herself into her room. Ginger was lying on the top bunk, reading. She glanced up as Mary-Kate threw her baseball glove on the floor.

"What's the matter?" Ginger asked.

"Nothing," Mary-Kate lied.

"Hmm." Ginger was silent for a minute. She seemed to be thinking. "Hey, guess what? Our math test was canceled. Mr. Surinam is sick, so we don't have to go to math tomorrow. Isn't that great?"

"I guess so," Mary-Kate said with a shrug.

"Well, have you heard the good news?" Ginger asked brightly.

"No. What?"

"Campbell has a date for the dance!" Ginger said. "She just called and told me."

Oh, swell, Mary-Kate thought. *Everyone in the whole school has a date! Except Ashley and me.*

But she was happy for Campbell. Sort of.

"That's nice," Mary-Kate said glumly. "Who's she going with?"

"Grant Marino," Ginger said.

"What?" Mary-Kate's mouth fell open. "Are you kidding?" she asked. "I thought *you* liked Grant—not Campbell."

Ginger looked puzzled. "Where did you ever get that idea?"

But Mary-Kate wasn't listening.

I don't believe it! she thought. *How could Campbell do that to me?*

How could she steal the one guy I like?

CHAPTER EIGHT

Mary-Kate ran out of her room. Her heart was pounding and her face was burning hot. She hurried through the lobby of Porter House, zooming for the front door.

"Mary-Kate? Isn't it a bit late to be going out?" Miss Viola called from the door of her room.

Miss Viola was the housemother. Her apartment was on the first floor of Porter House. She made sure the girls were all inside at 9:00, when they locked the front door.

Mary-Kate froze. "I'll be back in time," she answered. Her voice was shaking. "I'm just going next door."

"Well, don't be late," Miss Viola said.

Mary-Kate dashed out of Porter House and along the walkway leading to Phipps.

I don't even know which room Campbell has! she realized as she yanked open the other dorm's front door.

Inside, just off the lobby, a bunch of girls were gathered in the lounge. Mary-Kate poked her head in.

"Uh, does anyone know which room Campbell Smith is in?" she asked. "She just switched with Ginger Halliday. Jamie Randolph is her roommate."

"Upstairs. First door on the left," someone said.

"Thanks," Mary-Kate said.

Her throat started to tighten as she took the stairs two at a time.

What if she's not there? What if she's out for a walk or something?

Or what if she's on the hall phone right now—talking to Grant?

Mary-Kate got madder with every step.

By the time she reached Campbell's new room, she felt as if her blood were boiling!

Campbell was sprawled on a rug on the floor, reading her book for English.

"Hello, traitor!" Mary-Kate snapped, standing in the doorway with her hands on her hips.

Campbell's head shot up with a jerk. "Uh, hi. What's wrong with you?"

"Oh, nothing," Mary-Kate said. "I just can't believe you've stolen the only guy I really liked—that's all!"

"What are you talking about?" Campbell asked.

She dropped her book and sat up, cross-legged. She really did look puzzled.

"Don't play dumb," Mary-Kate cried. "I'm talking about Grant! You're going to the dance with him!"

Then she realized she was almost yelling. She checked over her shoulder to see if anyone had heard her in the hall. The coast was clear. "How could you?" she asked more softly.

"Why shouldn't I go with Grant?" Campbell answered. "You said *you* wouldn't go with him."

I did? When? Mary-Kate thought.

Oh, yeah. In the dining hall.

But that was only because . . . because she didn't think he would ask her!

Mary-Kate felt as if she were going to cry. She didn't want Campbell to see.

"I'm just saying that's not how roommates treat each other," Mary-Kate shot back. Her voice was still shaky. "Not if they're really friends."

Then she spun around and stormed out.

Her heart was still pounding as she started down the hall.

The last room on the right, near the stairs, was brightly lit. Mary-Kate could hear voices inside. Even before she got there, she recognized one of the voices. It was Dana Woletsky.

"I just figured, why wait for him to ask me?" Dana was saying. "So I asked him to the dance!"

"And he said yes?" another girl in the room asked.

"Yup. I'm going to the Spring Fling with Ross!" Dana announced.

Ross? Ross Lambert?

Oh, no! Mary-Kate thought. *This is the worst!*

She wanted to crawl under a radiator and hide.

She and Ashley had both been dumped by the guys they liked!

CHAPTER NINE

"Ashley!"

Ashley's head jerked up when she heard her name being hissed. Mary-Kate was standing in her doorway, out of breath. And her face was bright red.

"What's wrong?" Ashley asked.

Mary-Kate leaned into the room and glanced around. "Where's Phoebe?" she asked softly.

"Gone. She's studying with Wendy. Why?" Ashley said.

"Because I don't want to say anything in front of her," Mary-Kate explained. She came in and closed the door behind her. "I have terrible news."

What could be so bad? Ashley wondered. Did it have something to do with the All-Stars baseball team? Ashley knew that Mary-Kate had been practicing with the team earlier that day.

"I was just over in Phipps," Mary-Kate began. "And I overheard Dana talking. She and Ross Lambert are going to the dance!"

"Oh, no!" Ashley cried. "She's been trying to get him away from me all week! And it worked. He asked her out."

"No way." Mary-Kate shook her head. "From what I heard, she asked him."

That took a lot of nerve! Ashley thought.

But that was Dana. There was nothing she wouldn't do to get what she wanted.

"I can't believe it," Ashley said. "Dana and Ross are going together—to the biggest dance of the year! I'll be the only person in the whole school going alone!"

"No, you won't," Mary-Kate said. "I don't have a date either." She sat down on Phoebe's bed. "Grant asked Campbell to the Spring Fling. Can you believe that?"

Ashley's mouth fell open. "Campbell? Really?"

Mary-Kate quickly explained what had happened. Ashley saw how miserable she was.

"What are we going to do?" Ashley moaned. "We've been deserted!"

"There's only one thing to do," Mary-Kate replied.

"What?" Ashley held her breath.

"Get revenge!" Mary-Kate joked.

"Good plan!" Ashley agreed. At least it made her feel better to laugh about it. "I have an idea," she said, giggling. "How about if we sneak green food coloring into Dana's shampoo? We could do it next Saturday morning--the day of the dance. Then Dana would be too embarrassed to show up."

"Great idea!" Mary-Kate grinned. "Oh! I've got one! How about this? We make up some excuse to lure Dana and Campbell out of Phipps one night this week. If they don't get back to the dorm by Lights Out, they'll be grounded. Then they won't be allowed to go to the dance! Or the Lock-In!"

Ashley's eyes twinkled. "That's really too mean!" she said.

Mary-Kate flopped down on Ashley's bed and sighed.

Then Ashley saw Mary-Kate's eyes open wide. Her face was totally serious.

"What?" Ashley asked. "I can tell you've had a brainstorm."

"This is the best plan of all," Mary-Kate said, sitting up and leaning close to her sister, "because it could actually work!"

"What?" Ashley held her breath.

"What if we ask Dana to clean up all those weeds that are growing by the back door at the new Student U?" Mary-Kate suggested. "We could tell her the overgrown brush has to be cleared away so the back door can be opened during the dance."

"No way!" Ashley shrieked, laughing. "You know there's poison ivy growing there!"

Mary-Kate jumped up and danced around the room. "I know! Wouldn't that be perfect? Dana would be covered with poison ivy! Then she couldn't come to the dance!

Ashley laughed and threw a pillow at her sister. "I bet if we asked Campbell to help, she would. Then she'd have to stay home, too."

Mary-Kate laughed and headed toward the door. "Well, I feel better now," she said. "I guess I'll go back to my room"—she lowered her voice—"and face another night with poor, sniffling Ginger."

"Good luck," Ashley whispered sympathetically.

"Anyway, it was a kick to think about revenge," Mary-Kate said. "But we'd never really do anything, right?"

"Right." Ashley nodded.

We'd never actually *get revenge on Dana and Campbell,* Ashley thought.

Would we?

CHAPTER TEN

"Ross, could you help me?" Ashley called across the Student U.

Ross shot her a glare. "What now?" he complained, dragging his feet as he walked toward her.

Gosh, Ashley thought. Why was he in such a grouchy mood?

"All I want to do is move the couch to the other wall," she said.

"But I just moved it to *that* wall," Ross pointed out.

"Okay, so I've changed my mind a few times," Ashley admitted. "But we have to get the furniture right, so we have room for the dance tomorrow."

Ashley's throat sort of closed up when she said

that word. *Dance. I wonder if I'll actually get to do any dancing at the Spring Fling,* she thought.

"Do you need some help?" Mary-Kate asked.

Mary-Kate was working with Samantha and Phoebe on the decorations. They were hanging balloons from the ceiling and stringing small white lights all around the edges of the room.

"I think Ross and I can do it," Ashley answered.

She picked up one end of the couch—but it was heavy. The legs on her end barely left the ground.

Ross hefted the other end easily. "Talk about not carrying your share of the load!" he teased.

"I'm trying," Ashley said. She almost grunted as she struggled to haul the small leather couch to the far wall.

But it was too heavy.

She dropped her end with a loud *clunk*. Her side stuck out in the room. Ross's end of the couch was where it should have been—against the wall.

Ross laughed. "Is that where you want it?" he teased.

Dana laughed. "Very creative, Ashley," she called. "Yeah—I like it. We'll call it the Ashley Burke corner."

Ashley tossed her hair over her shoulder and tried to ignore the remark. She leaned against the couch and shoved it the rest of the way into place.

"Thanks," she said to Ross.

Ross didn't say anything. He just wandered back to where Dana was standing around. Dana muttered something in a low whisper. Ross laughed hard.

Great, Ashley thought. *I bet they're talking about me!*

At least the new Student U looked awesome. Ashley gazed around with pride. After all their work, it was almost complete. The walls had been freshly painted black and seafoam green and new lights had been installed—including the mirrored disco ball that Ashley wanted.

One back room held a couch, VCR, TV, video games, and lots of beanbag chairs. The other back room had the drink and snack machines. A folding rollaway Ping-Pong table stood against one wall in the big room.

And they had even raised enough money at the car wash to buy the second VCR that Ross wanted. It was in the big room, hooked up to a big-screen TV.

Best of all, the new furniture had been delivered! Ashley loved it.

The couches were really cool. There were lots of small love seats covered in salmon-and-white leatherette. They looked like they came right out of a 1950s Chevrolet convertible. And there was a really cool colorful rug in the middle of the room, for sprawling on.

"This place is so amazing!" Mary-Kate said. "I love it!"

"Great balloons," Ashley complimented her sister.

"Grant, can you hand me that masking tape?" Mary-Kate called from a stepladder.

Grant mumbled an answer. He handed her the tape without even looking her in the eye.

Wow, Ashley thought. Grant was being so cold to Mary-Kate! Ashley couldn't figure out why. Mary-Kate had always been nice to Grant!

And Ross acted totally icy toward Ashley. She could tell he thought she was bossy. But that was no reason to be so rude!

Going to the dance was going to be torture.

"We've got to roll up the rug," Ashley announced. She tried not to look in Ross's direction.

He looked annoyed anyhow. "I just got done unrolling it—right before you got here," Ross complained.

"Well, we have to roll it up again for the dance," Ashley explained patiently. She glanced around, looking for a place to put it. Mary-Kate was still on the ladder, so they couldn't move the rug yet.

"Over there in that corner," she said, pointing.

"But wait till Mary-Kate gets done decorating."

"Whatever." Ross turned away.

Ashley swallowed hard. She hated how Ross was talking to her. But she didn't want it to show. And most of all, she didn't want Dana to know she was jealous. She had better behave as if everything was okay.

Ashley stood and stared at the black wall. "You know, that was a great idea," she said to Ross. "One black wall. I'm really glad we went with it."

"You mean I did something right?" he said in a sarcastic voice.

Gosh! Ashley thought. Her face fell. *I'm trying to be nice, and he's yelling at me!*

Her eyes met Mary-Kate's.

Uh-oh, Ashley thought. *Mary-Kate looks mad!*

"Ross?" Mary-Kate called from the ladder. "There's still one thing you guys need to do. Why don't you and Grant go outside— and pull all those weeds that are growing by the back door!"

Oh, no! Ashley thought. *The poison ivy!*

"No!" she blurted out. "Don't do it!"

"Why not?" Ross snapped. "What's wrong—you afraid we won't do it right?"

Everyone in the room stared at Ashley. She gulped and said, "No that's not it. Mary-Kate doesn't know it but there's poison ivy out there and—"

"Come on, I'll help you, Ross," Grant interrupted her. He sounded grumpy. "Let's just do it and get it over with."

"No!" Ashley called again. "Let it go. We don't need to open that door."

But it was too late. The guys had already marched out the front door and around the building. They were pulling the weeds—with their bare hands and arms!

Yikes! Ashley thought. *They're going to be covered with poison ivy. And it will be all our fault!*

CHAPTER ELEVEN

"Where are they?" Ashley whispered to Mary-Kate.

Ashley glanced at her watch. It was 4:30 the next afternoon. Both sisters stood in the new Student U, setting up the table for refreshments. "Ross and Grant were supposed to be here an hour ago."

Mary-Kate gulped. "Poison ivy?" she guessed.

"That's what I'm afraid of," Ashley said nervously. "You never should have sent them out to pull those weeds."

"I know!" Mary-Kate buried her face in her hands. "But I couldn't help it. I just snapped when I heard Ross talking to you that way. He was being so . . . so mean!"

"Well, Grant was pretty cold to you, too," Ashley said. "Maybe that's why you snapped."

"Maybe," Mary-Kate admitted. She spread a paper tablecloth out on the table. Then she started lining up paper cups for the drinks. "But I'll still feel guilty if they actually get poison ivy."

"Well, maybe they're just sick of doing all the grunt work," Ashley said. She glanced at her watch again. "Do you think Ross and Grant would really just not show? I mean, if they were healthy, they'd be here—wouldn't they?"

Ashley bit her fingernail and glanced around. There wasn't much left to do. All the decorations were in place. The chips and snacks were lined up on the counter in the small back room. Everything was ready.

She looked at her watch again.

"That's the fourth time you've checked your watch," Mary-Kate said. "Give up. They're not coming."

"I know," Ashley said. "But how can we find out if it's because they're slackers—or because they're itching like crazy?"

Mary-Kate thought for a minute. Her eyes lit up. "Brainstorm," she said. "We'll call Jeremy. He can find out what's going on!"

Good idea, Ashley thought. Jeremy was their cousin and a student at Harrington. He could definitely find out if Ross and Grant had poison ivy.

The twins hurried back to Porter House. But there was only one phone in the dorm—in the hall. And seven girls were already waiting to use it!

"We made a sign-up sheet," Elise Van Hook explained.

"How come?" Ashley asked. "I thought we weren't allowed to do that."

"Miss Viola said it was okay, just for tonight—because so many girls want to call guys at Harrington. Everyone's trying to get a last-minute date for the dance tomorrow. Put your name here, and you don't have to stand in line for the phone." She handed Ashley a clipboard.

"Okay," Ashley said, signing her name. "Thanks. We'll wait anyhow."

Both girls sat down on the stairs. Forty minutes passed. Finally Elise called Ashley's name.

"Coming!" Ashley said, jumping up.

Mary-Kate followed her.

Ashley dialed the dorm at Harrington. She asked for Jeremy.

"Hi," Jeremy said. "What's up? You guys need dates for the dance or something?"

"No," Ashley said, talking softly so the other girls in the hall wouldn't hear. "Listen, we need a favor."

Quickly Ashley explained to Jeremy that she wanted him to go spy on Grant and Ross to find out if they were sick . . . or had any "rashes."

And she made him promise not to tell anyone why he was doing it!

"I'll hold," Ashley said. "Hurry."

Ashley tapped her fingers nervously while she waited.

"Are you talking or not?" a girl asked. "Because I'm next for the phone."

"I'm talking," Ashley said.

"Doesn't sound like it," the girl said.

"Okay, I'm waiting to finish talking," Ashley explained. *Hurry-up, Jeremy!* she thought.

"Hi," he finally said, back on the line. "Good news. Ross and Grant are fine."

"They are? I mean, no signs of . . . anything?" she asked.

"Like what?" Jeremy said. "I mean, they're both playing video games in the lounge. They don't look sick at all."

"They're not itching or anything?" Ashley whispered into the phone. "No signs of poison ivy?"

"Nope," Jeremy said. "Not that I could see. Why? What's going on?"

"Never mind," Ashley said. "See you later, okay?"

"Wait!" Jeremy yelled. "Don't hang up!"

"What?" Ashley asked.

"I heard you don't have a date for the Spring Fling," he said. "So I was wondering, do you want me to fix you up with Brian Maloney?"

Brian Maloney? Was he kidding? Brian was the creepiest kid at Harrington!

"No thanks." Ashley said. "Good-bye!" She hung up the phone and pulled Mary-Kate aside. "He tried to fix me up with Brian Maloney!"

"Ew," Mary-Kate said. "He must think you're desperate!" She leaned close to Ashley. "What did he say about you-know-who?" she whispered.

"Oh—they're fine," Ashley answered. "Nothing wrong."

"That's good," Mary-Kate said. "I guess."

The twins were quiet as they wandered back to Ashley's room.

"So why didn't they come to the Student U today?" Mary-Kate wondered.

"Because they didn't want to hang out with us?" Ashley guessed out loud.

Mary-Kate shrugged. "I guess so," she said softly.

"It's going to be no fun at the dance tomorrow night," Ashley said. "We'll have to watch them spend the whole night dancing with Dana and Campbell."

"No kidding," Mary-Kate said. "And then we'll probably have to spend the rest of the night at the Lock-In—listening to Dana talk about what a fabulous guy Ross is."

Yikes, Ashley thought. *That would be torture!*

In fact, it was more than Ashley could take.

"No, we don't," Ashley declared firmly.

"Huh? Why not?" Mary-Kate said. "What are you going to do—wear blinders and earplugs?"

"No," Ashley announced. "I'm not going to go. I'm going to skip the dance and the Lock-In altogether!"

CHAPTER TWELVE

"You guys are nuts," Phoebe said to Mary-Kate and Ashley the next night. "You're missing out on the biggest dance of the year! Are you really going to stay here? Alone? All night?"

"We're not alone," Mary-Kate joked. "We have Ginger."

She nodded toward her own room, down the hall.

"Oh, right," Phoebe said, rolling her eyes. "She's allergic to dancing or something?"

"Something," Mary-Kate answered glumly. "Anyway, she's staying in her room tonight. Our room, I should say. So we won't be alone."

"Whatever," Phoebe said. "But I still say you're nuts."

"We'll have more fun staying in," Ashley insisted. "We're going to make popcorn and watch movies all night."

"That's what we're doing at the Lock-In!" Phoebe reminded her. "At least you could come to that—when the dance is over."

"No thanks," Mary-Kate said.

She tried to sound okay about it, but it was a struggle. Missing out on a big dance was not Mary-Kate's idea of a great time. But she had decided to go along with Ashley. Neither girl thought it would be fun to go to the dance.

"Well, if you're not going, can I borrow your shawl?" Phoebe asked Ashley.

Ashley nodded and reached into her closet. Her black silk shawl with embroidery and fringe was hanging there.

"Yeah—this will look great with your black dress," Ashley said. "Here. Have fun."

"Yeah. You, too." Phoebe walked out the door.

Mary-Kate listened to Phoebe's footsteps on the stairs. They echoed because the dorm was so empty.

"This is the pits," she said when they were finally alone.

"I know," Ashley said. "It's so quiet in here! But I'm still glad we're doing it. I just couldn't stand to watch Ross dance with Dana all night."

"Ditto for Grant," Mary-Kate said.

"What? You think Grant will dance all night with Dana, too?" Ashley was trying to make a joke. But Mary-Kate could tell her heart wasn't in it.

Mary-Kate sighed. "Come on. We need a movie. Let's hit the student lounge." Mary-Kate jumped off Ashley's bed and headed for the door.

But Ashley didn't budge. "I've seen all the ones in the lounge," she mumbled glumly.

"Me, too," Mary-Kate admitted. She stood in the doorway, thinking. "I know! Ginger owns a copy of *Jaws*. We could watch that again."

"Okay," Ashley said with a nod. "It's better than nothing."

"I'll go get it," Mary-Kate said.

She slipped her feet into her slippers and padded down the hall. Ginger was sitting at her desk, writing a letter.

"Hi," Mary-Kate said. "Can we borrow *Jaws*?"

Ginger glanced up, as if she had been startled. "Uh, sure," she said. She stared at Mary-Kate's clothes. "But aren't you going to the dance?"

"Nope," Mary-Kate answered. "Ashley and I are boycotting it."

"How come?" Ginger asked. She swiveled in her

chair to face Mary-Kate, and gave her a worried glance.

Wow, Mary-Kate thought. *She looks like she really cares!* For the first time, Mary-Kate felt like opening up to Ginger. Maybe because the dorm seemed so lonely.

Or maybe it's because I miss Campbell, Mary-Kate thought.

Anyway, Mary-Kate decided to tell Ginger the truth.

"I just couldn't face it," she admitted.

"Face what?" Ginger asked.

"Grant," Mary-Kate answered. "You know how you kept asking me if I liked him? Well, I do. But he's taking Campbell to the dance instead."

"You're kidding!" Ginger's eyes opened wide. "Why didn't you tell me before?"

"Because I didn't want it getting all over school," Mary-Kate said.

"But he likes *you*!" Ginger almost squealed.

"He does? No way!" Mary-Kate said.

"Yes, he does," Ginger insisted. "He told Campbell that he liked you—and asked her to find out if you liked him. That was the day she moved into my old room."

"No way," Mary-Kate said again. But her heart

was beating fast. Could it possibly be true?

"Definitely," Ginger said. "But since Campbell wasn't going to be here to pick your brain, she asked me to find out if you liked him. That's why I kept asking you."

"Ohmigosh!" Mary-Kate blurted out. "I thought you were just being nosy!"

Or that maybe you liked Grant yourself, Mary-Kate thought.

Ginger flinched, but Mary-Kate ran over and gave her a hug.

"I'm sorry," she said. "I didn't mean it that way."

"That's okay," Ginger said. "I guess it did seem a little bit like I was just fishing for gossip. But I wasn't."

"Oh, no." Mary-Kate's eyes opened wide. She remembered what happened in the dining hall. "Campbell asked me about him, too."

"I know," Ginger said. "I heard all about it from Jamie. Anyway, Campbell told Grant what you said—that you wouldn't go to the dance with him if he asked you. That's why he finally gave up on you and decided to ask Campbell to the dance instead."

Mary-Kate's head was swimming. She didn't know what to say. So that's why Grant was acting so cold to her! He thought she didn't like him!

I've been such a jerk! Mary-Kate thought. *Especially for being mad at Campbell, who didn't steal Grant after all!*

"So anyway, you wanted to borrow *Jaws?*" Ginger asked, getting it from her bookshelf.

"No thanks," Mary-Kate said, snapping out of it. "But I wouldn't mind borrowing your earrings. I think I'm going to the dance!"

CHAPTER THIRTEEN

"Okay, I'll go to the dance, too," Ashley said when she heard the whole story from Mary-Kate. "But we're not staying for the Lock-In. Right?"

"Why not?" Mary-Kate asked.

"Because I still don't want to spend the whole night listening to Dana tell me how cool Ross is!" Ashley explained.

"Fine. Just hurry up and get dressed," Mary-Kate begged. "I'll meet you downstairs in ten minutes!"

Ashley glanced at her closet. The dress she had been planning to wear to the dance was hanging right in front.

Quickly she slipped out of her black Capri pants and into the little blue chiffon dress.

In two secs, she brushed her hair and tied it into a twisty knot on top of her head. She swiped some lip gloss onto her lips and added a small silver chain necklace.

Perfect! And in only 9.5 minutes—record time!

She met Mary-Kate at the bottom of the stairs. The girls knocked on Miss Viola's door to sign out.

"All right," Miss Viola said. "But if you're not staying for the Lock-In, I'll expect you back here by midnight."

"We'll be back," Ashley promised as they headed out the door.

The night was chilly, but the stars overhead twinkled brightly. Both girls walked quickly to get out of the cold. It wasn't far to the new Student U. Ashley could see the mirrored disco ball inside, twirling and sparkling with the music.

"I'm glad we're going," Mary-Kate said. "Listen to that! It sounds like everyone's having so much fun!"

"Easy for you to say," Ashley moaned. "Now that you know Grant likes you—you'll have a great time. Ross isn't talking to me."

Mary-Kate gave Ashley a little squeeze on the arm. "Come on," she said. "It'll be okay. I've got to find Campbell and apologize to her."

The girls stepped into the new Student U and gazed around. The dance was in full swing. But Ashley didn't see anyone she knew at first.

Then she made out a familiar face on the other side of the room. "There she is!" Ashley called out.

"What?" Mary-Kate asked, yelling to be heard above the loud music.

"There's Campbell," Ashley yelled back.

Ashley watched as Mary-Kate threaded her way through the crowd. Campbell and Grant were standing together on the far side of the room. Ashley couldn't hear, but she saw Mary-Kate take Campbell aside. The two girls talked for a minute, then hugged.

Good, Ashley thought. *They've patched it up.*

Just then Ashley felt someone tap her on the shoulder.

"Want to dance?" Brian Maloney asked her.

Ashley checked him out quickly. Brian looked a lot better than she remembered him. But she wasn't in the mood.

"Uh, I can't right now. I've got to talk to my sister," she told him.

Ashley slipped away and made her way around the edge of the room toward Mary-Kate and Campbell. But just as she got there, Mary-Kate and

Grant walked out onto the dance floor together.

That's great, Ashley thought. A slow dance was playing. She watched her sister dancing cheek to cheek with Grant. Mary-Kate wrapped her arms around his neck.

"Hi," Campbell said, smiling. "What's up?"

"You tell me," Ashley said. "It looks like you handed Grant over to my sister."

"I did. I didn't really want to be with him, anyway," Campbell said. "He's been talking about Mary-Kate the whole night."

"Really?" Ashley felt a little bit jealous.

"Yeah," Campbell said. "He really likes her. So I told them to go ahead and dance."

"That's so nice," Ashley said. But her face was sort of sad.

"What's wrong with you?" Campbell asked.

Ashley sighed. "Umm, I don't know. I just sort of wish I was here with someone," Ashley admitted.

"Who?" Campbell asked. "Anyone in particular?"

Should I tell her? Ashley wondered. *Oh, why not!*

"Ross," Ashley said, speaking into Campbell's ear. "But don't tell anyone. He doesn't like me. He likes Dana."

"Whoa!" Campbell said. She looked totally shocked. "You mean you don't hate him?"

Ashley shook her head. "Why would I hate him?"

"Well, it's just that I've heard Dana talking to him on the phone," Campbell said. "You know—she lives right down the hall from me in Phipps. She's been telling him stuff about you for the past two weeks."

"What? What kind of stuff?" Ashley demanded, grabbing Campbell's arm.

"Okay, I'll tell you," Campbell said. "But let's go outside. It's too loud in here!"

The girls slipped out the back door, and stood shivering in the cold. Quickly Campbell explained what she had heard Dana say to Ross.

"Dana kept telling him that you thought he was lazy," Campbell said. "And that you complained about his ideas for the Student U all the time, behind his back."

"I don't believe it!" Ashley cried. "She's such a liar! None of that is true!"

"Believe it," Campbell said. "I mean, two nights ago I heard her tell him that you spent the whole dinner hour dissing his taste in music."

"No wonder he's been so mean to me!" Ashley said, heading back inside.

"What do you think you're going to do?"

Campbell called, following her into the Student U.

"What can I do?" Ashley asked. "I can't tell him the truth. He'd never believe me. But at least I can get the disc jockey to stop playing that slow dance—so I don't have to watch Dana and Ross dance so close together!"

Ashley stomped through the crowd to where the DJ was sitting. She leaned over and shouted to be heard.

"Could you play something by 4 You next?" she asked.

"Sure," the DJ said. "What's your name?"

Why would he want to know my name? she wondered. But she told him anyhow.

"Okay," he said. "You got it, Ashley Burke."

A minute later, the slow song stopped. Ross and Dana were only a few feet away. Then a new song by 4 You started blaring out of the speaker system.

"This one is by request—for Ashley Burke," the DJ said.

Ashley blushed as a bunch of people turned to stare at her. *I'm not even dancing!* she thought. She felt totally dumb.

Then Ross caught her eye. He walked toward her. "You asked for 4 You?" he said. "I thought you hated them."

"No," she said, gazing into his eyes. "I love them. There are a lot of things I like that you don't know about."

Ross looked confused. "Really?" he asked.

Ashley nodded. "Dana has been telling you things about me that aren't true," she added. "In fact, I'll bet nothing she said about me is true."

Ross stared at her hard. Then he glanced at Dana. Then back at Ashley.

"Can we talk about this while we dance?" he asked.

"Definitely!" Ashley said, smiling so hard it almost hurt.

They stepped onto the dance floor and started moving to the music. But they couldn't really talk. The music was too loud. When the song ended, Ross reached out and grabbed Ashley's hand.

"Wait," he said. "Stay until there's a slow dance."

Ashley's heart flipped over. "What about Dana?" she asked.

"Forget Dana," Ross said.

Ashley saw Dana glaring at her and Ross. Then she whirled around and stomped away. She tossed her hair over her shoulders as she marched to the small room with the drink machines.

Then Ross took Ashley's hand and started dancing.

A slow song was playing. Ashley stood close to him and put her arms around his neck.

This is so cool! she thought. Ashley looked around the room. She saw Mary-Kate and Grant. They were slow-dancing, too.

"So you didn't tell Dana you thought I was lazy?" Ross asked. He reached up and scratched his neck.

"No way!" Ashley said. "You worked harder on this place than anyone."

"Not harder than you," he said. "I thought we made a great team."

He pulled her close to him.

Ashley beamed. This was a fantastic night!

When the song was over, they went to get something to drink. Then they played a few video games in the back room. And then they danced five more dances together.

Ashley couldn't believe it. And she couldn't wait to tell Phoebe and Mary-Kate all about it!

"Are you going to keep the disco ball going during the Lock-In?" Ross asked.

"The Lock-In?" Ashley's eyes popped. "I forgot about the Lock-In!"

"Huh? How could you forget about it?" Ross asked.

"Oh, Mary-Kate and I weren't going to stay for it," Ashley explained quickly. "We didn't bring our sleeping bags. What time is it—do you know?"

Ross glanced at his watch. "Eleven forty-five," he said. "The dance is almost over."

"Oh, no! Could you excuse me?" Ashley cried.

Ross nodded, and Ashley dashed across the room to find her sister.

"The Lock-In!" she said, grabbing Mary-Kate's arm. "We've got to stay for it!"

"But we don't have time to get our stuff!" Mary-Kate said. "They'll lock the doors of the Student U at midnight!"

"I don't care. We've got to try!" Ashley cried. "Come on—let's run!"

CHAPTER FOURTEEN

Mary-Kate said a quick goodnight to Grant. Ashley hurried to do the same with Ross. Then the girls raced out the front door of the Student U and ran across the dark campus.

"We'll never get back in time!" Mary-Kate called to Ashley, who was in the lead.

"We have to!" Ashley said. "I don't want to miss it. This is going to be the best night of the year!"

A few minutes later, the twins reached the front door of Porter House. They were both panting and out of breath.

"The door's locked!" Mary-Kate cried, pulling on the handle.

"Ring the bell!" Ashley said.

Mary-Kate pushed on the buzzer. Twice.

"Hurry up, Miss Viola," Ashley muttered.

Finally the front door opened. Mary-Kate ran in and took the steps two at a time.

"Ah. You just made it," Miss Viola said, glancing at the big grandfather clock in the lobby.

"We're going to go back to the Lock-In," Ashley said, talking fast and trying to get past the housemother. "We've got to get our sleeping bags and pj's. Excuse me, Miss Viola."

"Oh, no you're not!" Miss Viola said. "It's too late. You'll never get back there before they lock the doors."

Ashley glanced at the clock. It was five till midnight.

"Oh, please, Miss Viola! Please! We'll run!" Ashley said.

"No, I'm afraid not," the housemother said. "How will I know if you made it? I don't want you out there alone, especially if you're locked out."

But then Miss Viola glanced out the window. Her face changed. "Well," she said, "I see Fred, the night guard out there. Maybe he could escort you. And if the doors are locked—"

"Great!" Ashley said, dashing up the stairs before Miss Viola finished her sentence.

Ashley raced into her room, grabbed her pj's and sleeping bag, and ran out. She didn't even bother to put her pajamas in a tote. There was no time!

"Come on!" Ashley called to Mary-Kate down the hall.

"I'm already downstairs!" Mary-Kate yelled up from the bottom. "And look who's coming with us!"

Ashley almost slipped, she was running so fast to get down the stairs.

"Who?" she asked.

"Ginger!" Mary-Kate said. "Isn't that great?"

"Definitely!" Ashley said, giving Ginger a big smile.

"I'm sick of being sick," Ginger announced. "Who cares if I sneeze all night? I've got tissues."

"Way to go!" Mary-Kate said.

Ashley glanced at the grandfather clock. It said one minute till midnight.

Fred was standing in the lobby.

"Thank you, Miss Viola!" Ashley called as she raced past Fred, out the front door. "Come on, Fred!"

Fred laughed as he slowly followed the three girls into the night. "You go on ahead," he called. "I can see you fine."

That's what we were planning to do! Ashley thought as she started to run.

Both twins were dragging their sleeping bags and pajamas on the ground. But Ashley didn't care. She just didn't want to be left out of all the fun!

When they were only halfway there, Ashley heard the clock tower chiming.

Midnight.

No! she thought. *Don't lock the doors yet! Please!*

A minute and a half later, they reached the front door of the Student U. The building was still all lit up inside.

And the front door was wide open!

Mrs. Pritchard stood near it, trying to get the last of the boys to leave.

"Come on, boys!" she called. "The shuttle bus for Harrington is ready to pull away! Let's go!"

Ashley and Mary-Kate exchanged high fives.

"We made it!" Mary-Kate cheered.

"Yes!" Ginger cheered, running to catch up.

Ashley turned to wave at Fred. Then all three girls slipped inside.

"Well, hello!" Mrs. Pritchard said to them. "I'm glad to see you've decided to join us! You, too, Ginger. And congratulations, Ashley. Your committee did a good job with this building. You should be proud."

"Thank you. I am," Ashley said. When Mrs.

Pritchard turned away, Ashley leaned to whisper in her sister's ear. "Isn't this an awesome night?"

"Totally!" Mary-Kate said. "And it's just getting started!"

Ashley found a good spot for her sleeping bag near Phoebe's and spread it out on the floor. Mary-Kate put hers next to Campbell's.

Ginger hurried to find her old roommate, Jamie.

For the next few hours, the girls did nothing but talk about the dance. And eat! Ashley was starved. She gobbled down two pieces of pizza and drank two sodas. Then she started on the chips.

"Look at Dana," Phoebe whispered. "She's over there pouting—even though she's surrounded by all her friends."

"I don't even care about Dana anymore!" Ashley declared. "This was one of the best nights of my life."

When Ashley and her friends had all finished talking about the dance, they moved into the back room to watch a movie. Then they played a game of Truth or Dare. Then they started on the snacks again.

By five in the morning, Ashley was pretty tired. But she wasn't going to sleep. Not until the Lock-In was over!

She glanced at Mary-Kate, who was snoozing on her sleeping bag.

What a great night, Ashley thought.

Some of the other girls were sleeping, too. Ashley took out her diary and wrote in it. All about Ross, and the dance, and the Lock-In.

Then she lay on her stomach and watched the sun starting to come up.

This is the best, she thought. The only thing she could possibly complain about was her pj's. They were itchy. She reached down and scratched both arms.

But the more she scratched, the more she itched.

Maybe I'm allergic to my roommate, too! she thought. *Just like Ginger!*

Then she noticed Mary-Kate scratching in her sleep.

She was rubbing her arms, too. Ashley got up and crept over to Mary-Kate's sleeping bag. She stared at her sister's arms.

Oh, no! Ashley thought.

"Mary-Kate, wake up!" Ashley said, shaking her sister.

Mary-Kate slowly opened her eyes. "What?" she mumbled groggily.

"Bad news!" Ashley said. "I think we have poison ivy! Look at your arms. We probably got it from dancing with the guys!"

Mary-Kate sat bolt upright.

"You're kidding!" she said. She stared at her arms. They were both bumpy and red. Her eyes opened wide. "Oh, man. The guys probably have it on their necks. They're probably scratching right now, too!"

"Shhh!" someone scolded them from a sleeping bag nearby. "I'm trying to sleep!"

Ashley tried not to scratch. But her arms were driving her crazy.

"Oh, well," Ashley said. "I guess we deserve it."

"Yeah? Well, at least we aren't the only ones. Guess who else deserves it?" Mary-Kate said with a smile.

Ashley followed her sister's stare.

There, on the other side of the room, was Dana.

Lying in her sleeping bag.

Scratching!

ACORN

The Voice of White Oak Academy Since 1905

SQUEAKY CLEAN!

by Elise Van Hook

Watch out, Porter House! You have a new resident—and it's got a long tail and little gray whiskers!!

The new tenant—a mouse!—moved in a few days ago. She was first seen in the old storage building on the north end of campus. Mary-Kate Burke spotted the little squeaker during the clean-up session last week. Dana Woletsky immediately voted to set a mousetrap. But Phoebe Cahill, a long-time animal-lover, decided to catch the mouse instead. She set a "kind animal" trap—and brought the mouse to Porter House the next day.

Here's the problem. The door to the trap was loose—and the mouse escaped.

Now there's a mouse in Porter House!

Miss Viola was heard saying "It isn't the first mouse and it won't be the last." Other Porter House residents were heard to reply, "Eek!"

GLAM GAB

by Ashley Burke and Phoebe Cahill

Fashion expert Ashley Burke

What's the latest fashion trend? Beads, beads, beads! If your clothes aren't already bead-decked, don't worry. It's easy to add some beaded beauty to an old pair

of pants, a skirt, or even a scrunchie. Here's how:

You will need: 1) a piece of clothing; 2) a needle and thread to match the color of the garment; 3) beaded trim by the yard from a fabric store OR tiny beads and clear nylon thread from a crafts store.

If you are using beaded trim by the yard: Buy enough trim by the yard to go all the way around your skirt or pant legs, with one inch overlap.

Sew the trim to the hem of the garment, using matching thread. Begin and end near a seam. Overlap the trim and fold the top end under itself.

If you are using beads and clear nylon thread: Make a knot in the nylon thread and pull the thread through from the wrong side of the garment. Add a few beads and take another small stitch. Add a few more beads and take more stitches until you have gone all the way around.

To add dangling beads: Sew a few beads onto the hem of the garment, as above. Then string one inch of beads onto the nylon thread without taking a stitch into the

material. Loop the thread around the outside of the last bead to make a knot. Push the thread back up through the remaining inch-long section of beads. Now you have a beaded dangle. Continue sewing beads across the hem, adding one-inch dangles every half inch as you go.

Wear your beaded beauty to the Spring Fling and show everyone how cool beads are!

THE GET-REAL GIRL

Dear Get-Real Girl,
The girls who live in the room next door are driving me nuts. Every Friday night they order pizza for about ten girls. They crank the stereo so loud, I can't get any homework done! How can I make them quiet down?

Signed,
Cranky Neighbor

Dear Cranky,
Puh-lease! You're trying to do homework on a Friday

night? Get real! You aren't mad at your next-door-dormies for playing the

stereo too loud. You're jealous that they're having such a blast and you're not invited!

Instead of being a party pooper, why not offer to host the bash in your

room. That way you can clean up the pizza crumbs for a change. And don't forget to invite the girls who live on the other side of you, too—or you'll be reading another letter just like this in my column next month!

Signed,
Get-Real Girl

Dear Get-Real Girl,
A few weeks ago this guy from Harrington asked me to the Spring Fling. I said yes because I figured no one else would ask me. Now a different guy wants to ask me to the dance. Guy #2 is sooo cute! How can I get out of the first date?

Signed,
Desperate

Dear Desperate,
There's a really easy way to get out of the first date. Just tell everyone that you were willing to dump one guy for another—and no one will want to go out with you!

Seriously, it's not worth treating guys like dirt

unless you're willing to be treated the same way in

return. So keep your promises and go with Guy #1. But that doesn't mean you can't dance a few times with Cutie #2. Just remember: Hands off Cutie #47. He belongs to me!

Signed,
Get-Real Girl

THE FIRST FORM BUZZ
by Dana Woletsky

Well, you know spring has arrived when the gossip is flying as fast as the pollen here at White Oak!

For starters, has anyone noticed that all the daisies on campus have been plucked? Someone whose

initials are AB is playing the "He likes me, likes me not," game. Or did her twin sister pick all the daisies? Hard to tell them apart—since they're both losing in the dating game these days!

We have one big winner on campus, though. A certain girl from Porter House recently moved into Phipps—and she wins my award for Most Boring Wardrobe! Seriously, CS, how can you tell your pj's from your

day clothes? Try wearing something other than a baseball jersey for a change!

The hottest rumor of the week is about SS, who claims she can't sit down

in class this week because she hurt her back in a soccer game. But the real scoop is that she stayed under her tanning lamp so long, she burned the backs of her legs to a crisp! I told you it was a hot rumor!

That's it for the buzz. Remember my motto: If you want the scoop, you just gotta snoop!

ALL-STARS SHINE IN STELLAR BALL GAME

by Mary-Kate Burke

Sports pro Mary-Kate Burke

Let's hear a cheer for the White Oak/Harrington All-Stars baseball team! We beat the Danville Day School 3-2 in extra innings last Saturday—a game that is sure to become a White Oak legend.

Both teams came out swinging in the first inning. Danville was up by one when yours truly stepped up to the plate—and slammed a homer!

The score was 2-2 for the next nine innings! The crowd was tense until

Grant Marino stepped up to bat at the top of the tenth. We held our breath. And he slammed another home run straight over the fence to win the game!

Coach Fisher gave Grant the MVP award. And one of his teammates (I'm not saying who) was heard to say, "Hey—he'll always be the Most Valuable Person as far as I'm concerned!"

UPCOMING CALENDAR
Spring/Summer

Take the plunge and come out to cheer for all those cute Harrington guys at

their final platform diving meet on May 5. It's a totally wet and wild event! (Can anyone say Speedos?)

Don't tell the ants . . . but everyone else is invited to the end-of-school picnic

on May 29! There will be a prize for the winner of the pie-eating contest. Dress for a mess!

Time to pack it in! Remember: you must have your clothes packed to ship home by

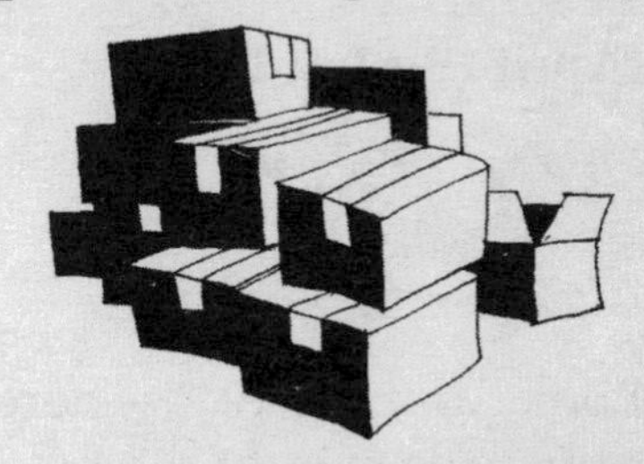

Friday, May 25. Need extra boxes? Don't go postal! Just ask Mr. Frangianella for help.

Something's fishy in the Florida Keys! Find out about a cool summer program, swimming and snor-

keling till your skin turns wrinkly! Info meeting on Saturday, May 5, in the new Student U. Be there—and you'll get hooked for sure!

It's All in the Stars
Spring Horoscopes

Taurus

(April 20-May 20)

Look out, world—here comes the sign of the bull! You're a powerhouse of strength, Taurus. That means you can master anything you decide to tackle this month. Just remember that you can be a little bit stubborn and bull-headed at times—even with your closest friends. Make sure you leave room for someone else's opinion once in a while.

Gemini

(May 21-June 20)

As the school year ends, it's time for a change. How about taking up a new hobby, getting a different haircut, or trying a new food? Take a risk this summer: Learn how to juggle, do a back dive, or stand on your head. You'll be surprised how great it feels to look at the world from a different angle!

Cancer

(June 21-July 22)

Your sun sign says you're ready to kick back, relax, and have a rock 'n' roll summer! And hey—that's totally you. You're solid as a rock and always ready to roll with the punches. No wonder your friends like to lean on you. But remember you don't always have to be the strong one. It's okay to depend on somebody else from time to time.

I was so grateful I leaned over and gave Devon a big hug. I expected him to blush but he didn't. In fact, the only person turning deep red was Ross!

And if he didn't suspect before that I like Devon—he sure does now!

Dear Diary,

I may be snug in my bed now but just hours ago I was in the middle of a mucky, yucky swamp!

The minute Phoebe, Elise, and I stepped into our canoe I knew there'd be trouble.

"Stop shaking the canoe!" Elise demanded.

"How can I stop shaking the canoe when I can't stop shaking myself?" Phoebe cried.

Phoebe was dressed in vintage army camouflage. She wore a 1940's hat on her head with a net to cover her face.

"No way am I getting a mosquito bite," Phoebe told us. "I know all about malaria."

Our canoe drifted through swamp grass and soupy water. I sat in the bow of the canoe, which meant I saw everything first. Every bug. Every snake. Every horseshoe crab.

The swamp got narrower as we paddled. Soon the other canoes were out of sight.

We were totally alone.

"This hanging moss is gross!" I said, brushing it aside. "And what's that glittery stuff coming up?"

"Glittery?" Elise gasped. "Where?"

Elise loves anything glitter. But as we grew closer I was pretty sure she wouldn't love this.

I gasped as layers and layers of spider webs seemed to dip lower and lower. With big yellow-and-black spiders!

"Tarantulas!" Phoebe cried.

We ducked but it was no use. The spider webs practically brushed our heads.

"Little Miss Muffet was right," I shouted. "I'm out of here!"

"Where are you going?" Phoebe demanded.

I looked around. There was a tiny, mossy island about fifteen feet away.

"There!" I said.

"I'm right behind you!" Phoebe declared.

Phoebe and I swung our legs over the canoe.

Stop!" Elise shouted. "You can't swim in the swamp!"

"Why not?" I asked.

"Hel-lo?" Elise asked. "Haven't you ever heard of alligators?"

Phoebe and I both froze.

Alligators?

HarperEntertainment
Outta-site! marykateandashley.com Register Now
The New Adventures of
MARY-KATE & ASHLEY
Check out the
Trenchcoat Twins'
NEWEST ADVENTURE!
Collect your own Mary-Kate & Ashley photos! Look inside!
The Case Of The
Logical I Ranch
Coming soon wherever books are sold!
TWO of a kind Diaries
First in a Special Two-Part Series!
Shore Thing
The Diaries of Mary-Kate & Ashley!
Hang out with
Mary-Kate & Ashley
. . . read their next
TWO OF A KIND book!

- ❑ The Case Of The Great Elephant Escape
- ❑ The Case Of The Summer Camp Caper
- ❑ The Case Of The Surfing Secret
- ❑ The Case Of The Green Ghost
- ❑ The Case Of The Big Scare Mountain Mystery
- ❑ The Case Of The Slam Dunk Mystery
- ❑ The Case Of The Rock Star's Secret
- ❑ The Case Of The Cheerleading Camp Mystery
- ❑ The Case Of The Flying Phanto
- ❑ The Case Of The Creepy Castle
- ❑ The Case Of The Golden Slipper
- ❑ The Case Of The Flapper 'Napp
- ❑ The Case Of The High Seas Secr
- ❑ The Case Of The Logical I Ranc

Starring in

- ❑ Switching Goals
- ❑ Our Lips Are Sealed
- ❑ Winning London

HarperEntertainment
An Imprint of HarperCollins*Publishers*
www.harpercollins.com

eading Checklist

ndashley

ingle one!

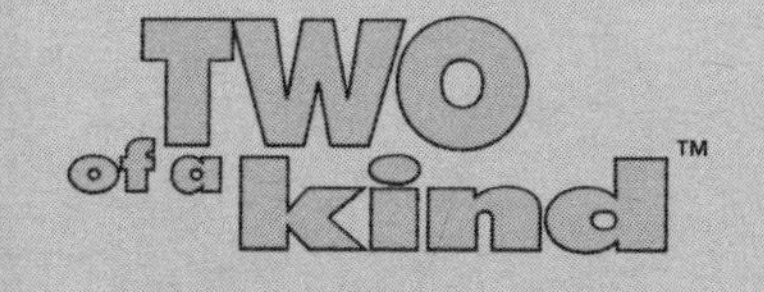

- ❑ It's a Twin Thing
- ❑ How to Flunk Your First Date
- ❑ The Sleepover Secret
- ❑ One Twin Too Many
- ❑ To Snoop or Not to Snoop?
- ❑ My Sister the Supermodel
- ❑ Two's a Crowd
- ❑ Let's Party!
- ❑ Calling All Boys
- ❑ Winner Take All
- ❑ P. S. Wish You Were Here
- ❑ The Cool Club
- ❑ War of the Wardrobes
- ❑ Bye-Bye Boyfriend
- ❑ It's Snow Problem
- ❑ Likes Me, Likes Me Not

Super Specials:

- ❑ My Mary-Kate & Ashley Diary
- ❑ Our Story
- ❑ Passport to Paris Scrapbook
- ❑ Be My Valentine
- ❑ Wall Calendar 2001

Available wherever books are sold, or call 1-800-331-3761 to order.